This book belongs to

To weather watchers
and cloud spotters

Thank you to
Kallie George
and meteorologist
Phil Chadwick

Tundra Books, an imprint of Penguin Random House Canada
Young Readers, a Penguin Random House Company

Library and Archives Canada Cataloguing in Publication
MacKay, Elly, author, illustrator
  Red sky at night / Elly MacKay.
Issued in print and electronic formats.
ISBN 978-1-101-91783-1 (hardcover).—ISBN 978-1-101-91785-5
(EPUB)
  I. Title.
PS8625.K38845R43 2018   jC813'.6
C2017-902902-9 C2017-902903-7

Published simultaneously in the United States of America by
Tundra Books of Northern New York, an imprint of Penguin
Random House Canada Young Readers, a Penguin Random
House Company

Library of Congress Control Number: 2017940264

Edited by Tara Walker
Designed by Kelly Hill
The illustrations in this book are photographs of paper dioramas.
The text was set in Yana.
Printed and bound in China
www.penguinrandomhouse.ca

1 2 3 4 5 22 21 20 19 18

Penguin
Random House

tundra | TUNDRA BOOKS

SOURCES

Books
Bowen, David. *Weather Lore — Guide to Weather Quotes,
Sayings and Proverbs*. Hob Hill Books, 2013. eBook.

Day, Cindy. *Grandma Says: Weather Lore from Meteorologist
Cindy Day*. Halifax, NS: Nimbus, 2013. Print.

Lalonde, Shirley. *Never Sell Your Hen on a Rainy Day: Weather
Signs, Rhymes and Reasons*. Kelowna, B.C.: Sandhill, 1998. Print.

Stackpole Books, eds. *Survival Wisdom and Know-How*. New
York, NY: Black Dog & Leventhal, 2007. Print.

Websites
Environment and Climate Change Canada:
Sky Watchers' Guide
https://ec.gc.ca/meteoaloeil-skywatchers/

The Old Farmer's Almanac
https://www.almanac.com

Royal Meteorological Society
http://www.metlink.org

UCAR Center for Science Education
https://scied.ucar.edu/webweather

RED SKY AT NIGHT

ELLY MacKAY

tundra

WEATHER FOLKLORE

Long ago, here and far away, people looked for clues in nature to predict the weather. They learned from experience by watching the shapes of clouds or noticing the behavior of animals. This wisdom was passed down through sayings like the ones in this book.

How weather-wise are you?

Might you know a saying or two?

Red sky at night, sailor's delight.

When the dew is on the grass,
no rain will come to pass.

Evening red and morning gray,
two sure signs of one fine day.

When the mist creeps up the hill,
fishers, it's time to try your skill.

No weather is ill if the wind be still.

If woolly fleeces are in the sky,
be sure the day is fine and dry.

When ladybugs swarm, expect a day that's warm.

When the wind is from the West,
then the fishes bite the best.

Yellow streaks in a sunset sky,
wind and daylong rain are nigh.

Frogs will call before the rain,
but in the sun are quiet again.

Whether it's cold or whether it's hot,
we shall have weather, whether or not.

Ring around the moon, rain will come soon.

Red sky in the morning, sailors take warning!

Trout jump high when rain is nigh.

Hear the whistle of the train?
'Tis a sign it's going to rain.

Winds of the daytime wrestle and fight,
longer and stronger than those of the night.

Wind from the East
is neither good for man nor beast.

Little ships must keep to shore.
Larger ships may venture more.

If seabirds fly to land,
there truly is a storm at hand.

When clouds appear like rocks and towers,
the Earth is refreshed with frequent showers.

Cats leap about and chase their tails
to warn of thunderstorms and gales.

When the forest murmurs and the mountain roars,
close the windows and shut the doors!

The more rain, the more rest.
Fair weather's not always best.

Now that you know a saying or two,

can you predict what the weather will do?

Weather sayings have deep roots. Before people could check a weather report, they kept a close eye on the sky and watched the behavior of animals to predict approaching storms. Reading the skies meant they could bring a boat back to land or take animals to a safe place before the weather changed. There are many versions of these sayings. Some sayings in this book have been updated in order to be passed on to younger generations, though the messages remain the same. Their accuracy may vary depending on season or location, but all are based on observations from nature and share valuable weather wisdom and a connection to the past.

Red sky at night, sailor's delight.
True (in temperate zones). In some parts of the world, the saying goes, "Red sky at night, shepherd's delight." But whether you are on the sea or in the meadow, red skies (but not red clouds) at sunset mean there is calm air in the western sky. By the next morning, that nice weather should be right overhead.

When the dew is on the grass, no rain will come to pass.
Usually true. If there is dew, it means there was a clear sky throughout the night. Of course, it doesn't tell us how long the clear skies will last!

Evening red and morning gray, two sure signs of one fine day.
Usually true. Dew and low-lying fog, or mist, makes everything look soft and gray. Like dew, fog may appear after a cloudless night when the ground is cool. The water droplets soon evaporate when the warmth of the sun heats the air.

When the mist creeps up the hill, fishers, it's time to try your skill.
Usually true. Mist rises when there is warm air and sunshine, so it's a perfect time to go fishing.

No weather is ill if the wind be still.
Not always true! While this saying is often true in the summer, you may also have heard people warn about "the calm before the storm."

If woolly fleeces are in the sky, be sure the day is fine and dry.
True. Woolly fleeces, like sheep? Yes! Cumulus clouds look like big fluffy sheep. These clouds are also known as "good weather" clouds because they are usually accompanied by sunshine.

When ladybugs swarm, expect a day that's warm.
True. Ladybugs will only fly in warm weather and become very active when they get too hot. They collect heat under their shells and release it by flying.

When the wind is from the West, then the fishes bite the best.
Somewhat true (in temperate zones). Western winds bring the fairest weather, so it may be the nicest time to be out in a boat. Another version of this saying goes, "The wind in the West suits everyone best."

Yellow streaks in a sunset sky, wind and daylong rain are nigh.
True. Cirrus clouds look like "yellow streaks" at sunset. The Latin name for these clouds mean wispy hair, which is just what they look like. These clouds are a sign of changing weather. "Nigh" in this saying means coming soon.

Frogs will call before the rain, but in the sun are quiet again.
Questionable. While animal behaviors can be observed, they are hard to prove scientifically. One explanation for hearing loud croaks before the rain? The croaks sound louder because sound travels better in humid air.

Whether it's cold or whether it's hot,
we shall have weather, whether or not.

True! This we can depend on. Weather is always changing, from day to day and throughout the year. The air that surrounds our earth is always being heated or cooled, resulting in wind, clouds and precipitation (such as rain, hail, snow and sleet).

Ring around the moon, rain will come soon.

Usually true. A halo (or ring) around the moon appears when there are cirrostratus clouds, which are very high clouds made of ice crystals. They are a sign that the weather is changing and there might be rain coming.

Red sky in the morning, sailors take warning!

True (in temperate zones). If you see a red sky in the morning, it means calm air has already passed over you and stormy weather will be coming. Red clouds aren't a great sign either. They mean you likely have a low-pressure system already overhead. If you are a sailor, prepare for a storm or head to shore!

Trout jump high when rain is nigh.

True. When there is low air pressure, it usually spells rain. Before the rain comes, insects fly low, looking for cover. Minnows, on the other hand, come to the surface of the water, following the rising gas bubbles that have been released by the low air pressure. If you are out before the rain, you might see fish jumping to catch the low-flying insects or in pursuit of the minnows.

Hear the whistle of the rain? 'Tis a sign it's going to rain.

True. Sound travels better through air with high humidity. When there is moist air and cloud cover, the sound waves travel along the surface of the water or ground instead of scattering upwards.

Winds of the daytime wrestle and fight,
longer and stronger than those of the night.

True (except behind a cold front). At night the air is cool, but when the sun heats the air in the daytime, warm and cool air mix, creating wind.

Wind from the East is neither good for man nor beast.

True (in temperate zones). In places like North America or Europe, where winds usually move from west to east, eastern winds bring cold and storms. Animals can sense a change in the air pressure before storms arrive. Some people can, too, complaining of aches and pains in their joints.

Little ships must keep to shore. Larger ships may venture more.

True. Little ships are advised to make their way to a safe port when there are warning signs of an approaching storm. Large ships are more stable in rough waters.

If seabirds fly to land, there truly is a storm at hand.

True. Seabirds are very sensitive to changes in temperature and air pressure. By instinct they know when a storm is approaching. The sea can be quite nasty when the weather turns, so seabirds will come to shore to seek shelter.

When clouds appear like rocks and towers,
the Earth is refreshed with frequent showers.

True. High, towering clouds are called cumulonimbus clouds. Their name means heaping storm clouds in Latin. If these clouds darken and you hear thunder, head for cover!

Cats leap about and chase their tails
to warn of thunderstorms and gales.

True. While cats aren't great weather forecasters, sailors used to watch their behavior closely. Have you ever had your ears pop? Your ears are adjusting to a change in air pressure. Cats are much more sensitive and have been seen to act nervously and hide when the air pressure drops. Sailors took this strange behavior as a sign of a coming storm.

When the forest murmurs and the mountains roar,
close the windows and shut the doors!

True. Sound travels better before a storm. If you hear the sound of wind in the distance, prepare for a storm.

The more rain, the more rest. Fair weather's not always best.

True. When these sayings were common, the rain was a welcome rest for the many people who used to work outside, often from sunrise to sundown.

Elly MacKay is an acclaimed paper artist and children's book
author and illustrator. She wrote and illustrated the picture
books *If You Hold a Seed*, *Shadow Chasers* and *Butterfly Park*,
among others. Elly's art was also featured on the covers of
Tundra Books' reissues of L. M. Montgomery's Anne of Green
Gables and Emily of New Moon series. Her distinctive pieces
are made using paper and ink, and then are set into a miniature
theater and photographed, giving them their unique three-
dimensional quality. A member of the Cloud Appreciation
Society, Elly lives in Owen Sound, Ontario, where she watches
the weather with her husband and two children.